Metanoia

A. Awana

<u>*Metanoia,*</u> *(Greek)*

(n.) The journey of changing one's mind, heart, self or way of life.

Or

Beyond/After Thought

Note from the Author

Dear Readers,

All these poems are very dear to my heart. It took me around eight months to come up with the complete book. At first, I should confess that I never was a poet. I might have written poems but then neglected the idea because of my obvious reasons that 'I was not a poet.' I always wrote stories because it is one of the many things that I love the most. But all my stories remained somewhat unfinished and now when I look back, I think and believe that things were meant to be this way only. I was supposed to find something that I can give my whole heart to, where all my faith, dedication comes align, to that particular thing in which I can grow and evolve. And, that thing is poetry. It gave my mind a new direction, not only to move forward, but also to see things differently.

This book was supposed to be out in the first week of September, but things didn't work out the way I had planned, so the date was moved forward. But, I believe it is okay as long as I am satisfied with my work. Being a novice in the field, I don't have any confidence, but only faith.

I hope you, the readers, would love it, and if not love, then I can manage with like too.

Thank you.

Content

To

The one

Who is Afraid

And,

Wants to be

Brave.

Black & Blue

One soul,

Two shadows,

They walk side by side.

This story isn't romantic,

If you want me to emphasize.

One is called blue,

And the other is called black,

Both are the daughters of Jack.

One had to sleep under the bed,

Or inside the closet.

Black is stubborn,

She doesn't follow orders.

Blue is submissive,

Doesn't care about others,

If someone took away the closet and bed,

What the other will do?

Fight for each other,

Or let it doom.

They are sisters they should help each
other.

When black was attacked,

Blue said she is not strong enough.

When blue was attacked,

Black said that act didn't catch her eyes.

Both are killing each other,

Destroying,

Tormenting,

Bit by bit.

When the sun shined on her eyes,

She saw the light,

Turned away to look around for blue,

She knew that she wasn't true.

<u>Different Place</u>

If I tell you,

There is a different place,

Where lies have an important place,

Where everything is learned,

Only to be used,

Feelings are only the cues,

Where stars shine differently,

I could easily call them mine,

But it might take me a fortune.

Nobody stops,

If there isn't a need,

They would love to walk,

But only with materiality.

A place,

Where knowledge is shared,

With alikes only,

No concerns are for the outlaws.

Who thinks differently.

No questions are asked,

Only answers are available,

A place,

Where thundering sky,

Became the muse,

Of the literary elites.

Truth is,

What they won't choose.

Now it is up to you,

What will you choose?'

Prayers

Every night,

While

I sleep,

I try to keep,

You in my prayers,

Not because,

I care,

But because

There is something,

I cannot say,

Cannot say it aloud,

Aloud to you.

You may ask,

What do you mean by,

'To be in the prayers',

Then I would tell you,

It doesn't always have to be for the good,

It is my god,

I can ask,

Whatever I want.

I can ask,

To help your soul,

To give you everything,

That you hope for.

I can ask,

For you to have a good fortune,

A good wealth,

And good health,

I can ask,

Nice people to surround you.

I could ask for anything,

And all these things,

That I wish for,

Might come true,

But I won't.

I won't,

Because

There are certain things,

That you cannot keep control of,

You only think,

Good things are meant to be in prayers,

But when your heart is pure,

Good things are not always what you ask
for,

I could ask,

To torment your silly soul,

Or

Unrest your deceiving mind,

Or,

Restlessness,

For your wicked heart.

Haven't I told you,

I could ask for anything,

But I won't,

But,

I promise you,

I will keep you in my prayers,

Where I will ask my god,

To give you everything,

Not what you asked for,

But what you deserve,

If merit is the thing,

According to which your worth,

Will be weighed,

Because in the end,

It is only your heart,

Which will keep you in this game.

Breathe

If you insist

I should tell you,

Here live a million things,

That your eyes cannot see,

Thousand lives,

But nobody really dies,

It becomes lighter when your breath goes
away.

But let me just tell you there are a million
other ways.

Your heart can always be in denial,

The truth that you cannot accept,

The light you cannot see,

Always lost in a thought,

What your life would be?

One single deep breath,

Gives you a lot to think.

If it is me,

I would rather not take one,

But many.

I believe and you should too,

Life is a waste,

If you don't gather thoughts,

That can help you.

Lady of the Tower

In the big tower,

Outside the town,

There lives a lady.

She never goes out,

Doesn't know anybody.

Rumour circles the town,

That,

She is a witch

She has big turquoise eyes,

Long black hairs,

That touches the ground.

One said I saw her talking to a bird

After that,

My vision got blurred.

One said I saw her flying in the sky.

I thought maybe I should also try,

Maybe she could teach me,

To walk on water,

I can take up the role of her daughter.

I could learn to make gold from sand,

So together we can make nature's law amend.

I took up the road which led to the tower,

Only to attain,

Power.

I reached the land,

And I saw the fences,

They were beautifully crafted,

I thought she indeed is a witch,

She transformed the old barren land,

Into a magnificent tower.

I tried to get in,

But the lady caught me,

Asked me 'what's the matter?'

'I am here to meet the lady of the tower',

She smiled and said,

'The lady is me and

The tower is here,

Are you not afraid,

Or should I make you a deer?'

'Others are afraid,

This is the reason,

Why I came.

I want to be the same as you,

Who can fly,

Whenever she wants.

Walk on the water,

Over, the currents.

May I be the one in your favour?'

'You think very highly of me.

But,

I don't fly but heal the flying birds.

I don't walk on water but water my plants

I don't ride the currents but swim according
to it.

I am nothing but an ordinary person.'

I got puzzled,

And asked her,

'I do have a query?

Would you mind to answer it?'

'Why not, child'

'They fear you,

When you do nothing extra-ordinary,

Being powerless,

How you manage?'

'Oh, my dear,

You are very naive,

Don't you know the system?

In this world,

When a woman lives on her own,

She becomes a witch.

A man who tries to do something different

Becomes, a coward.

This is the rule of the land,

Which everyone blindly follows.'

'Then I will follow you,

And would love to be a

Powerless witch.'

<u>*Evolution*</u>

Evolving is a process but most of us believe it is a miracle.

<u>*Ignorance*</u>

Why don't you come outside?

Don't you feel lonely?

Staying all day by the cupboard side.

See the shining chandelier,

It is brighter than the sun.

Have you seen the sparkling lights?

That adorns the sky.

You know there lives a lady across this
room,

She shines like glitters,

She is light as feathers,

Her voice is sweeter than the nightingale.

She always circles the room in her vintage
dress,

She looks perfect.

I don't know what to do to make her
impress.

I pity you,

And I hope,

You remain ignorant.

The chandelier isn't brighter,

Stars are only balls of fire,

And the lady,

Is always restless.

She circles the room to escape,

Her vintage dress is all she has.

Feathers are always broken,

And her voice is shaken,

By the horrors she holds.

Indeed she looks perfect,

With all her scars.

Don't bother to impress,

She doesn't care,

We all are the pawns,

In the big game of chess.

<u>*Materiality*</u>

Don't get swayed by

What you see.

Even the sand glitters

In the night,

And,

Stars disappear

When the dawn arrives.

<u>Hopeless Soul</u>

The hopeless soul,

Always asks others for help,

And,

When they do,

The hopeless soul,

Tends to forget,

Whatever the soul achieves,

It's his to call,

And the part of miseries,

Comes in others fold.

Cruelty

You always tell me,

The reason for your cruelty.

You are always in fear,

Always afraid,

But if I could,

I would tell you,

Your feelings are not even near.

Being afraid does not mean

Hating

Judging

Cursing, others.

But

It does every cruel thing to the self.

You & Devil

The Devil that stays by your bed,

Never seems to go away.

Because you are the one,

Empowering him,

Feeding him,

On your fear.

It is you,

Who got accustomed to his presence,

Its absence makes you feel empty.

The void you feel,

Makes you restless,

Leads you,

Towards,

Self-destruction.

Words are not feelings

I saw,

You were standing in front of me,

So close,

Yet,

It felt so far.

Your eyes fixed on mine,

You gazed deeper,

As if you are trying to hypnotize,

But you shake your head,

Like every time,

Is it so hard to understand?

You always tell me,

You love me,

But why do I feel,

The words are not feelings?

I feel like it is not enough,

Not because,

It is not enough for me,

Because

The love you give others,

Has raw emotions,

While

The part of love I get,

I feel like it is filtered.

I don't know,

What do you feel about me?

But,

I believe,

From your side,

It is always going to be a mystery.

And,

I am not that hard to read.

But,

The only thing you are lacking,

Is the ability to try.

It feels like,

I always throw a thread towards you,

So that we both could stay in tune,

But,

You drop the thread,

You don't realize that the thread,

Is the only thing,

By which we both are sticking.

And if,

I ask you about the matter,

Then you will say,

I am making an excuse.

But truth,

Is what it is.

You even know it better.

Darkness

Take my hand,

It will help.

I am no different,

From the one you fear.

Yet,

Don't be afraid.

This is a decision you need to make.

In the dark,

You cannot see,

But can open your eyes.

While in the strongest light,

Every effort goes to waste,

When you try,

It only hurts.

And,

Leaves you,

With nothing,

But pain.

Lies

Do you know where the truth lies?

Not inside your smiles.

But under your thousand lies.

When you try to hypnotize me,

With your creamy words,

You shoot them like arrows,

While I act like a target,

I can see through it,

But, still choose to follow.

Sometimes,

I wonder,

You are tricking me,

Or

I am fooling you,

Or is our greed making us,

Deceive each other?

Hazel

If I had to define colour Hazel,

That would be very normal.

It seems pretty ordinary,

From afar it seems,

Similar to brown.

But when you get closer,

You always get drowned.

In the depth it holds

The beauty it reflects.

Makes you wonder,

What really it has?

And makes you believe,

Beauty is in the simpler things.

<u>*Story*</u>

A story,

Where the king loved the throne,

More than his queen.

A story,

Where the queen aimed higher

Than being the mere mother of an heir,

A story,

Where an heir,

Tried to save the country.

A story,

Where the queen slashed,

The head,

Of a greedy king.

A story,

Where an heir left the palace,

To keep his citizens at peace,

A story,

Which became a historical piece.

Down the lane,

Of the history,

Where the greedy king,

Became the helpless puppet.

Who gave up his life,

On his own free will.

The ambitious queen,

Became the vicious witch,

And,

The peacemaker heir,

Who gave away the throne,

For the people of the country,

Became a coward.

Path

If jealousy is what you feel,

While being on the right side,

Then I must correct you,

You are no longer right.

It might give you pain,

But never jealousy,

It makes you warm,

But only enough to keep you alive,

When you start burning from inside,

It is not the warmth of righteousness,

But the fire of deceiving,

First,

It will give you,

An enormous power,

You will feel like you can uproot the world,

Then it will burn you down,

Down to the ground,

And,

Your worth will be no more than ashes.

<u>Humanity</u>

They told humanity is for love,

If you don't have it,

You are no human.

But what I believe is,

Humanity can hate too,

And so has envy,

Persuasion is present,

While

Manipulation is the key.

Humanity has every emotion

With equal proportion.

The only thing humanity posses,

Makes it so amiable,

Is its ability to

Learn and transform,

For a Better Future.

Rebirth

When you start understanding

And

Stop judging,

You are reborn with a new vision.

You understand that everyone are just
humans,

The things that hurt you,

Affects them too.

Scars that scares you,

They feel it too.

Chills run through their spine too,

When,

They encounter something dangerous.

Their heart flutters just like yours,

And sometimes skips a beat too.

They are no different from the

One, who live insides you.

The soul that ignites you,

Runs them too.

Courage

They told me,

'Your courage,

Is in the middle of the ocean,

If you want to find it,

Buckle up for the adventure.

There will be storms,

Sirens and ships.

A little bit of ice too.

Various hardships,

You have to go through.

While I can only advice,

You have to embark this journey,

On your own,

No ally,

No assistance,

I can provide.'

I thought a little bit,

I realised,

'Me' is all I have,

And courage will be all I need,

Let's start this journey with hope.

I found some ships,

They were not interested,

Encountered storms,

Made my hair all fussy,

But I always wondered,

Where the sirens will be,

I saw none,

This made me a little grumpy.

But,

The hope of finding my courage,

Was brighter than the feeling of
disappointment,

In the middle of the ocean,

I found a glittered blue box,

I jumped with joy,

Inside it,

I found a small scroll,

In it,

It was written,

'Inside every being, there lies courage,

One only has to find it'

Berries

I asked him,

'Where are you going?'

'Down the hill,

To bring you the berries.'

'Try to find the blue ones,

I would like to make fruit jam.'

'Anything else Madam!'

He replied sarcastically,

He has always been a blissful child,

But I never knew,

What was under his smile?

I never made the Jam,

He never came back,

Though,

The town down the hill,

Remained bustling with people

Thought I should go,

Look for him,

I wondered for a bit,

Even after all these years,

He remained just a stranger,

What good will do I get?

To find him,

Maybe,

He always wanted to keep me at bay.

<u>Night</u>

On a rainy night,

There is only one hope of light,

The thundering sky.

<u>Expectations</u>

You should not hate,

You are not supposed to be jealous,

Should try to accommodate,

But do not try to be too comfortable.

These words echo in my ears,

Got imprinted in my mind.

Your double standards,

Drips from your tongue,

Reflects your thoughts.

This made me hate you more,

More,

You will never know.

<u>*Let's meet on the other side*</u>

'Let's meet on the other side.'

You told me,

But,

What if there is no other side?

What if,

The other side is nothing

But a lie,

Or

Another shithole,

Where we will be trapped

For another life.

An unknown place,

Where maybe I won't remember you,

Or

You won't remember me,

And all these things,

Will put another baggage on our sufferings,

Or,

Maybe there is no side at all,

The only thing we have is this,

When people fail to accept the truth,

Lie is what they choose,

Lie,

To relieve their agonizing souls,

To reignite their hopes,

That they will accomplish the half-done
things,

On the other side.

The myth,

That we hold onto,

The hope,

That we can complete our desires,

On the other side.

But the truth is hidden,

And,

The reality is unknown.

Still,

We try to keep going,

And,

Dreaming,

All the things,

We don't even know of.

<u>Wrath</u>

One day they threw a feather,

I did not respond,

I did not think further.

Again they threw a pebble,

It hit the mark,

But I let it drop.

Again they threw a stone,

I resisted with a tough tone.

Again they threw a pot,

This time,

I made them run.

But they came back again,

To drown me.

But I was smart,

I know how to swim.

This time I did not wait,

I went to their place,

Burned their city down,

They shouldn't have messed around.

<u>Warmth</u>

I have always been cold,

Never knew what really warmth was.

When I found you,

You gave me what I needed,

It felt good.

You took me in your embrace,

With you I found peace.

As I never knew the feeling,

I didn't realise,

Slowly I was burning,

Down inside to my core,

In the next moment.

I was one of the ashes.

Warmth II

If I ever get a chance,

I want you to know,

I never meant to burn you down,

I was as naive,

As you were.

In my, own happiness,

I forgot,

What you were going through

You didn't knew the warmth,

And,

I didn't knew the nature of my warmth.

I didn't realise when it became fire,

Strong enough to pull you down,

Down with the ashes.

<u>*The smoke*</u>

The smoke that I see,

Is coming from your burnings.

The fire inside you,

Has already unleashed its terror,

And,

Now,

Your soul has started to quiver.

It is only a matter of time,

When,

We all will see,

Who is beneath your skin,

An angel or demon,

Who breathes.

Or,

You are just,

Too good at pretending.

Burned Soul

Let's say,

I am the one,

Who burned your soul,

I will accept,

All the allegations,

You will put on me.

I will happily keep,

All the stains,

You will throw on me.

And,

I will make sure,

I will be punished,

And,

You get what you asked for.

But,

In return,

I want to ask you a favour,

I hope,

You could do,

This bit to me.

You believe your soul,

Was an angel,

Who was not meant to be

Part of the dirt,

But,

You do tell me,

Was I the one,

Who threw you into the dirt?

You believe,

Your soul was pious,

And,

You alleged,

That mine was,

Filled with sins.

But,

Please,

Try to tell me,

When you are so naïve,

How did you learn to differentiate between things?

You believe,

I burned your soul,

But do you really,

Believe,

I was the one,

Who set your soul on fire?

I accept,

Your allegations,

But,

For your wellness,

My voice should be heard,

You were sitting on the pile of coal,

With a tiny void in your soul,

The fire in your heart,

Burned your soul,

As you used coal,

To complete your soul.

Hide & Seek

In this modern world,

In the name of modern love,

We hide the truth,

And,

The lie is what we seek.

<u>*Owe*</u>

You told me,

'I will always be on your side,

It doesn't matter

If you are wrong or right'

I believed every word,

You told me.

Saw everything,

You showed me.

I closed my eyes,

Followed you everywhere.

You drove me to the brink,

Suddenly,

Left my hand,

And,

Told me,

'I don't owe you anything'

I looked around,

I laughed at myself,

By looking how far I had come

I replied,

'You owe me the trust,

I gave you.

The faith,

I had on you.

And time,

I invested in you.

You owe me everything,

In this world,

Everything,

That you can never repay.'

Heart

Let me give you a warning,

Never wear your heart

On your sleeve.

As others will see,

Where it bleeds.

They will know where the hole is.

Keep it safe inside,

Where all the secrets hide.

Because nobody put bandages,

But they always put spice.

Angel & Human

I fell in love with an angel,

Being the one,

He cannot reject my loving heart,

As that will be a sin,

Which,

He doesn't want to commit,

Or,

Harm.

On,

The other hand,

I was a human,

And being one,

I neglected his sufferings,

Did everything,

To keep him,

All to myself.

I wonder,

Why we are so crazy about possessions?

Why possessions become our passion?

Why letting go,

Is so hard to get,

The ability that our hearts

Always forgets.

They say,

Love is all about sacrifices,

Which I don't want to make.

I am getting to keep,

The one I love.

Then I don't know why?

But,

I am in pain.

Being with an angel,

I learned the ability,

Of loving someone else,

Other than me.

And,

Being with a human,

He learned the ability,

Of committing sins.

Home

You smell like a raging fire,

Your heart seems like a battlefield,

You look like a torn soldier,

Who is tired,

Wants to go home,

Or a place,

Which is better than home.

Neutral

The world that we live in,

The world that we dream of,

Both are made of neutral energies.

Sun shines,

Gives us the heat we need,

On the other side,

The moon shines too,

But has nothing of its own,

Relies on the sun,

And,

Is as cold as ice.

But its beauty,

Catches everyone's eyes.

<u>*End of the World*</u>

What if the world ends today?

Would you still fight,

To keep me at bay,

Or,

You would find me,

Or secure your place.

If the civilization end today,

And,

We no longer,

Be the part of the cradle,

Would you still choose,

To walk over me,

Or would choose,

To walk with me.

When the new life,

Will began,

Where there will be no traces,

Of not mine,

And,

Not yours.

The world,

Would be different,

So different would be scriptures.

What if,

The fiction that you read,

Will become,

Tomorrow's history,

Black magic would not be,

So wicked,

Or for better,

Could become a part of new science.

A world,

Where trying something,

Could be encouraged,

Where loving,

Somebody,

Would never fill others with rage.

A world,

Who understands,

This world's fears,

A world,

Where people would hear,

To pleas,

To miseries.

A world,

Where soul,

Could be in peace,

And not fill with,

Agony.

Afraid

I cannot restart,

There is an unknown ache in my heart,

Fear runs in my veins,

I don't know,

How to take it straight?

If only I am not afraid,

I would make a better aim.

Black hole

I am in this big black hole,

The harder I try,

To get out.

The deeper I fall,

Inside it.

It is like it's a never-ending game,

And,

I am only waiting for the Judgement day.

Hopes

In another world,

I hope,

There is a sky,

Which will be livelier,

Not only birds,

But everyone,

Could call the open sky

'A home'

But I wonder,

What if then,

We will wish for a livelier land?

Horns & Feathers

Sometimes I doubt,

These societal measures.

They tell us,

Horns are for demons,

While

Angels have feathers.

But what I perceive,

Over the years,

Aren't horns supposed to be strong?

They denote power.

Feathers are fragile,

They don't look so strong.

How I am supposed to take it,

When I feel this is wrong.

I do understand it,

What you feel now,

I have felt the same way too,

Maybe,

It is the cycle of life,

That we all go through,

Horns are powerful,

But they don't know,

How to change their way,

They are stubborn,

When it comes to make a way.

But feathers are delicate,

Makes way for a new life,

Or are even ready,

To make a flight.

Things are not always the way we tell them,

But what they hold,

Is what makes them.

Enough

Let's try to be enough.

Be enough,

For each other.

Instead of copying each other,

This time,

Let's try to cope with each other.

Dream

Last night I had a dream,

That,

We could see nothing,

We could only hear things,

All the faces just dissolved,

As if they were made up of sand,

Dripping from the hand.

But I could hear,

Everything you said,

Clearly.

Understood your laughter,

Vividly.

If only,

I could understand it better,

When I had you,

The pain you were in,

Never caught my eyes.

The isolation you felt,

Never crossed my mind.

I always tried,

To ease my mind.

But your uneasiness,

Always stayed aside.

And,

Now,

When there is nothing left of yours,

Which I could call mine,

I understood everything,

All the things that you never said,

Or things that you thought,

Were better left unsaid.

When I know,

You are a matter of the past,

And could never be in the future,

I still hope,

For you

There might be a place,

Where you don't have to be a part of the
race,

A place where being true should not be the
only case.

A place where your presence could be
praised,

And,

A place where I could be in your prayers.

Pride

Because of your hopeless pride,

Every day,

My dreams die.

The more proud you become,

My wounds become deeper,

Your eyes surely can see them,

Every inch of it,

But you try to hide,

From my wounds,

From my hurting,

And, From

Your, own feelings.

<u>*Plants*</u>

It seems like,

I am watering the dead plants,

For so long,

That I,

Myself have forgotten,

What a living plant looks like.

Words & Meanings

You never know,

What one really means,

Because one word,

Can have different meanings.

At this place,

You need a correction,

As,

It is us,

Who are complicated,

One word,

Always have one meaning,

And,

It is only us,

Who interpreted them with feelings.

Hierarchy

I woke up,

Under the water,

I was amazed to see the view,

The water was brighter,

Inside the ocean,

And I could breathe too.

I could swim,

You know,

What is even better,

I could fly too.

My body became lighter,

With every stroke I made.

I swam with the fishes,

Saw different plants.

But there was no sign of land.

I tried to swim up,

Cut through the ocean,

I followed the light,

But,

There was some inside my eyes.

I lost track of time,

The light went out,

I wonder why longing of land,

Troubles my mind.

I would try again,

When the next light arrives.

Till then,

I wonder,

Does hierarchy in the water exist?

If it does,

Where my place is?

My well trained human mind,

Did not recognized,

That they might not have a hierarchy,

Based on some material needs,

But,

On who could hunt better,

Or

Who have better canines,

Or

Better natural weapons.

Or,

Even better,

They do not possess,

Any knowledge,

To divide the living type,

No society they would believe in,

They just remain,

As they are,

Kill when they need,

Till then,

Does not pay any heed.

Society,

Is for humans,

They live in the world.

<u>*Change*</u>

You told me,

You have changed,

Even though,

You haven't aged.

There are certain things,

I want you to know,

All my life,

I have always been the same.

It was only you,

Who has a lens in the eyes,

Always focus on,

What you really,

Want to see.

Not me,

But you are the one,

Who makes reality lie.

But,

I always wonder why?

<u>*Love & Hate*</u>

Isn't it a weird world,

We live in?

We give everyone hate,

They don't deserve,

But love,

Only to chosen ones.

It is so easier to hate someone,

Even one look is enough.

While

Loving somebody is a tough job.

And,

Now I understand,

Why we only talk about,

Spreading love,

Because

Love is what we all lack,

On the other side,

We all have hate in abundance.

Which we don't even try to hide,

Everything is at the forefront.

Gratitude

All these times,

I was only juggling the hopeless balls,

Running around in never-ending hoops,

To find one thing,

That will make me,

More of a person,

Who will be needed,

By the ones,

Who I need.

If only,

You could understand,

That my love for you,

Is never going to vanish,

But in the end,

It can never surpass,

The weight of gratitude,

That my heart holds,

In this battle,

I see no scope.

Gratitude,

Is not something

That could be weighed.

Initially,

I have already lost the game.

But I will not leave the field,

As you know,

Love is not always about gains,

Its value lies in our faith.

The battle is not lost until,

The soldier decides to call it off.

You don't understand a thing,

It is not a fight,

You are doing nothing,

But wasting your time,

I am not worth

The wait.

You are not a soldier,

And

I am not waiting for a triumph.

I wonder sometimes,

How one decides,

The worth of one,

Isn't it only a matter of the heart?

Why your mind intervenes?

The person who is dear to your heart,

Could be a villain to someone else,

Then how that person's worth

Will be matched.

You only think of yourself,

Be considerate of others too.

Everybody's life is not a theoretical formula,

That you could jump through.

Indeed,

Every person's life cannot be weighed,

But in my case,

I don't know

How long will be the wait.

If you think,

I am being selfish,

Let your mind be so.

Conclusion is all,

What we draw,

But I don't know,

If I am the one,

In your heart,

Or all the feelings,

Were only of the name.

Just stop for a moment,

Think about me too.

Do you really think,

'I don't want you'?

You might not be the best,

But,

If it is you,

I will leave the best.

It's just the circumstances,

Which are making me mad.

If gratitude is a thing,

That is pressing your heart,

Let's share the weight.

And,

If the wait is a thing that you want,

Then I am ready to wait for an eternity

But the fire,

Burning inside my heart,

Will never fade,

Because

I believe,

That my love will never fail.

Acknowledgement

I would like to thank to all my friends and family, who supported me. And I would also like to thank my god who helped me and gave me confidence.

This book's cover page's art and design is taken from Adobe Spark Post. All copyright belongs to them.